The Adventures of Commander

Zack Proton
and the Warlords of Nibblecheese

By Brian Anderson
Illustrated by Doug Holgate

Aladdin Paperbacks
New York • London • Toronto • Sydney

This one is dedicated to everybody who bought the first Zack Proton book and helped launch Zack, Omega Chimp, and FE-203 into the universe. —B. A.

For my cats. Who if it wasn't for me wouldn't be fed. —D. H.

ALADDIN PAPERBACKS
An imprint of Simon & Schuster Children's Publishing Division
1230 Avenue of the Americas, New York, NY 10020
Text copyright © 2006 by Brian Anderson
Illustrations copyright © 2006 by Doug Holgate
All rights reserved, including the right of
reproduction in whole or in part in any form.
ALADDIN PAPERBACKS and colophon are
trademarks of Simon & Schuster, Inc.
Designed by Sammy Yuen
The text of this book was set in Zolano Serif BTN.
Manufactured in the United States of America
First Aladdin Paperbacks edition October 2006
2 4 6 8 10 9 7 5 3 1
Library of Congress Control Number 2006925725
ISBN-13: 978-1-4169-1365-8
ISBN-10: 1-4169-1365-3

CONTENTS

CHAPTER ONE

Time 2-B a Hero

Commander Zack Proton stared in disbelief at the cockpit computer screen. The entire Oortian armada was racing after Captain Carnivore's ship and gaining fast.

Captain Carnivore was hopelessly outnumbered, and his supplies were running low. If he was captured, he'd spend the rest of his life trapped in some underground Oortian rock mine. There was only one thing to do.

"Attack!" Zack shouted. He grabbed the game controller and stabbed at the fire button. He zigged and zagged using the joystick. Captain Carnivore's ship zipped in and out between enemy fighters until there was a flash of light and the screen suddenly went red. The words YOU ARE SPACE TOAST appeared in white letters. PLAY AGAIN?

"Captain Carnivore never accepts defeat!" Zack said, and clicked YES to play again. At that moment a blue light began flashing in the cockpit. Beep! Beep! Beep!

"Omega Chimp!" Zack called. "Will you turn off this annoying distress signal? I'm trying to play a game here!"

Omega Chimp rushed to the cockpit and scanned the computer readout. "It's a class two-B distress signal coming from the Zeta Quadrant," he said.

"Class two-B doesn't sound very serious," Zack said. "Can we get back to my game now?"

"A class two-B signal means an entire busload of second graders is in immediate danger."

"Immediate? You mean right now?" Zack asked. Omega Chimp nodded, and Zack jumped to his feet. "Leapin' leptons, man, what are you waiting for? It's time to be a hero! We've gotta save those students, protect those pupils, rescue those . . . wait a minute. How long is this going to take? Because aren't we supposed to be looking for my ship?"

It's true that Zack and Omega Chimp had been searching for Zack's spaceship, the Risky Rascal. And the sooner they found it, the sooner Omega Chimp could get Zack Proton and that defective robot droid, FE-203, off his own ship. But an emergency distress signal always came first.

"This should only take a minute," Omega Chimp said. "Those old school bus ships are always breaking down. They probably just need a tow to the nearest fuel station."

"Great! I'll unplug Effie from the recharger," Zack said, already dashing toward the back of the ship.

"No need!" Omega Chimp called. But it was too late. Omega Chimp shook his head and set the ship's controls to take them to the Zeta Quadrant. With any luck they would resolve this minor emergency in no time and quickly resume their search for the Risky Rascal.

Crash! Tink-tink-tink. Ker-thunk!

"It's okay," Zack called from the back of the ship. "Nothing's broken."

"Except—"

"Quiet, Effie!" Zack snapped.

Somehow, Omega Chimp knew this rescue mission wasn't going to be that easy.

CRASH!

COMMANDER ZACK PROTON

HEY, WAIT A PARSEC! WHO ARE THESE GUYS?!

HEAVE

STRUGGLE

ARE WE STARTING? *WAIT*, I'M NOT READY!

...GENUINE INTERGALACTIC SPACE HERO AND CAPTAIN OF THE *RISKY RASCAL* —

— UNTIL HE FELL OUT THE BACK DOOR OF HIS SHIP INTO SPACE.

SOMEBODY GIMME A HAND OVER HERE, WILLYA? OMEGA CHIMP, *HELP!*

LUCKILY FOR ZACK, OMEGA CHIMP WAS PASSING BY IN HIS OWN SPACESHIP.

WHAT? I CAN'T HEAR A THING WITH THIS HELMET ON.

I SHOULD HAVE JUST KEPT GOING.

TOGETHER THEY SET OFF IN SEARCH OF THE *RISKY RASCAL*

TOSS

SPLAT

HELLO? OMEGA CHIMP? ARE YOU STILL THERE?

AND THE SOONER WE FIND IT, THE BETTER.

SOON THEY ENCOUNTERED AN ABANDONED FE-203 ROBOT DROID ORBITING A FROZEN PLANET...

COMMANDER PROTON *RESCUED* ME!

EFFIE? IS THAT YOU?

...AND WERE ALMOST *KILLED* TRYING TO RESCUE THE PLANET POTLUCK FROM THAT VICIOUS SPACE GIANT, *BIG LARGE!*

OH YEAH, I REMEMBER THAT! SORRY FELLAS!

KEEP PULLING, EFFIE. IT'S COMING OFF!

TUG

WHERE ARE WE? WHAT'S GOING ON?

WRAP IT UP, YOU TWO. WE JUST REACHED THE ZETA SECTOR. IT'S TIME TO GET BACK TO THE STORY.

POP!

QUICK! WHERE'S MY HELMET?

CHAPTER TWO

Ring Around the School Bus

Omega Chimp slowed the Giant Slayer as they neared their destination. Through the windshield they saw a school bus spaceship completely surrounded by dozens of tiny alien warships.

"Cheese-wedge fighters!" Omega Chimp cried in horror. "You realize what this means?"

"Lunch break?"

"It's the warlords of Nibblecheese!" Omega Chimp answered.

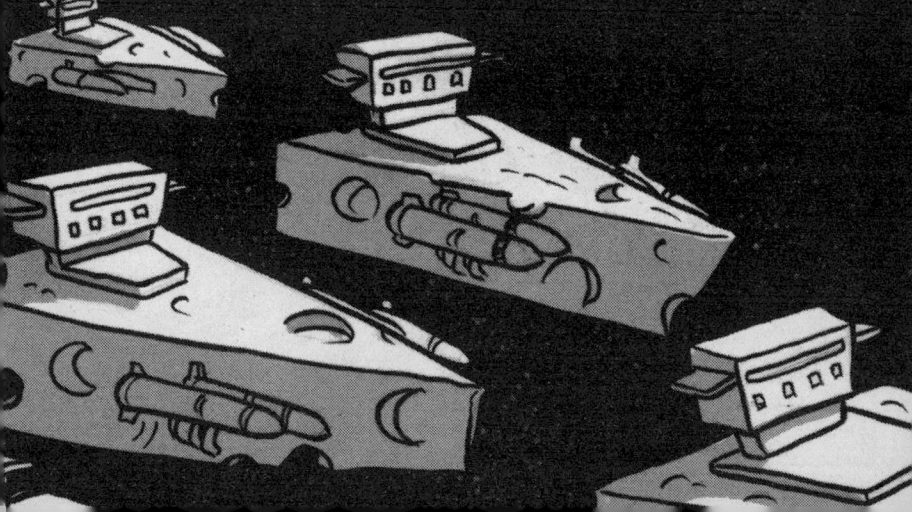

"Oh, I remember," Zack replied. "They're a ruthless horde of giant rodents who invade every corner of space, trying to make the universe a better place for mice. I saw a holovid program about them."

"You watched an educational show?" Omega Chimp asked.

"I had to," Zack answered. "I couldn't find the remote control."

Effie used his telescopic vision to get a closer look at the bus. "Commander Proton! That's an Earth bus!" he said.

"But what could the warlords of Nibblecheese possibly want with a busload of Earth children?" Omega Chimp wondered.

"Their interest in Earth can mean only one thing," Zack said. "They're planning to conquer the moon!"

"The moon?"

"All that green cheese would feed millions of space mice for years," Zack explained.

Omega Chimp rolled his eyes. "Green cheese. Of course. Why didn't I think of that?" he said.

Zack continued excitedly. "Say, do you think planets are also made of cheese? I'll bet if you dig deep enough . . ."

"Is that what they're teaching in school these days?" Omega Chimp asked.

Zack shrugged. "Don't ask me," he said. "I don't even know what they were teaching when I was there."

Important Health Bulletin: If you find a piece of green cheese in your refrigerator, throw it away. It is not a moon rock.

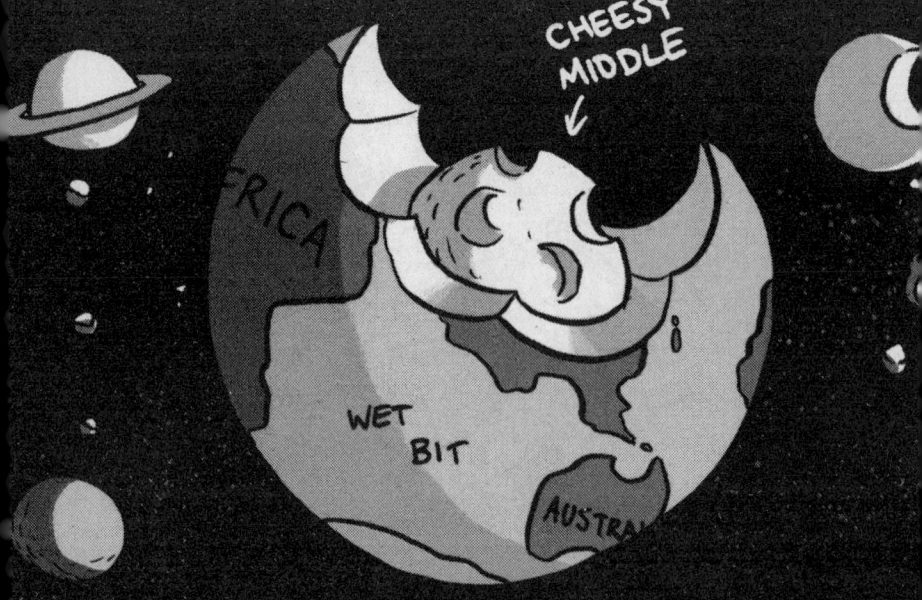

CHAPTER THREE

A Full Spectrum of Trouble

Zack couldn't wait to try out their brand-new Ion Scrambler 3000 transporter device. Used properly, it would teleport them from Omega Chimp's ship to whatever destination they chose, instantly and painlessly.

Zack set the controls for the nearby school bus and reached for the transporter button.

"Zack, wait!" Omega Chimp cried. "We haven't tested it yet, and we're not wearing our wristbands, and—"

Zack tapped the transporter button three times. An outline of pulsating rainbow light appeared around each of them.

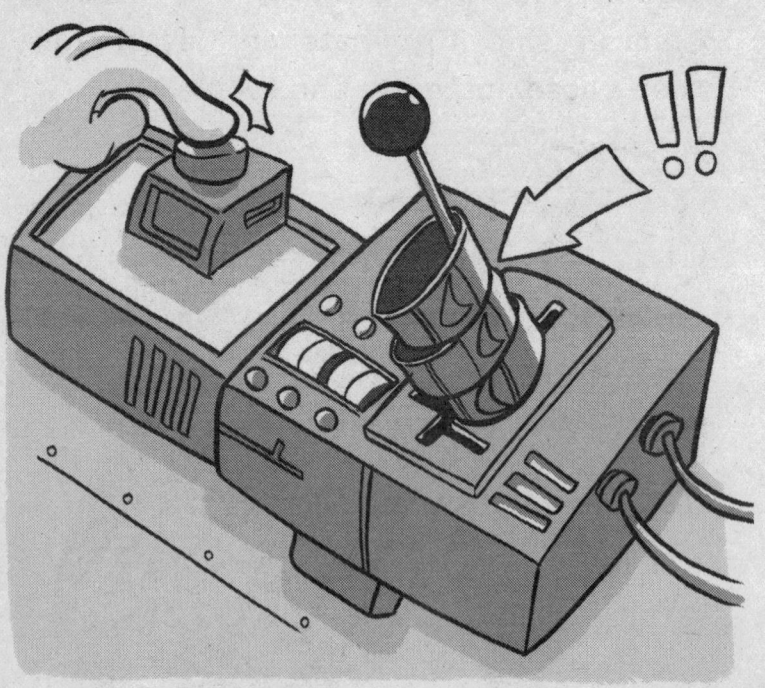

"This is wild!" Zack said. "It reminds me of the time I sneaked into the control room at the Klaatu Memorial Test Rocket Facility. Every time I pushed a button, the whole room glowed a different color."

"That was you?! Every rocket crashed that day! My flight was delayed for six months!"

The rainbow light surrounding them suddenly grew brighter, and a high-pitched whine filled the cockpit.

Effie started singing, "'Daisy, Daisy, give me your answer, do! I'm half crazy, all for the love of you! . . .'"

"I think something's wrong with Effie," Zack said.

"Something's wrong with me, too," Omega Chimp moaned, clutching his stomach.

At that moment the rainbow outlines flashed, and Zack, Omega Chimp, and Effie vanished.

In the past school buses were a primitive, uncomfortable, and unreliable way for students to travel on field trips.

CAN'T YOU WAIT TILL WE GET THERE?

CLANK
CLANK
CLANK

Today's modern school buses are nothing like the ancient land buses. These technological marvels allow the teacher to continue her lessons while traveling to the destination with all the comforts of a regular classroom.

25

"Are we there yet?"

"Only ten million miles to go."

"Are we there yet?"

"Just nine million miles more."

"Are we there yet?"

"Be quiet."

"Are we there yet?"

"Stop that right now or I'll turn this bus around and bring you straight back to school! All right, that's better. . . ."

"Are we there yet?"

CHAPTER FOUR

Take Me to Your Warlord

Zack, Effie, and Omega Chimp appeared in a flash of light on the school bus ship. "It worked!" Zack cried. "What were you two worried about?"

Effie rolled back and forth on the floor, his lights flashing randomly. "Error . . . error . . . error . . . ," his mechanical voice repeated. Omega Chimp just lay on the floor, his whole body curled up into a ball. His eyes were closed, and he was moaning like an out-of-tune choirboy.

"Are you here to save Miss Canterbury?" a boy asked.

Omega Chimp forced one eye open and looked up. They were surrounded by twenty sad-eyed children. He pushed himself slowly to his feet.

"Canterbury?" Zack asked. "Why does that name sound familiar?"

"She's been taken prisoner by those wicked mousemen," a girl added.

"Well, if she's anything like my old second-grade teacher, Miss Craterbrain, you kids are better off without her," Zack said.

"But we like Miss Canterbury."

"You like your teacher?" Zack asked, confused. "In that case, of course we'll get her back. When we find those warlords of Nibblecheese, why, we'll rout those rotten rodents, we'll mash those miserable mice, we'll vanquish those vile vermin!"

ZACK PROTON'S TIPS FOR YOUNG SPACE HEROES

Tip #1: A bold and rousing pep talk helps encourage your followers and makes them respect you.

"I don't think finding them will be any problem," Omega Chimp said.

"Why not?"

"Because we're standing right behind you!" squeaked an angry little voice.

Zack turned around. A squadron of mouse warriors armed with swords and ray guns glared furiously at them.

ZACK PROTON'S TIPS FOR YOUNG SPACE HEROES

Tip #2: A badly timed pep talk can also enrage your enemies and make them attack you.

CHAPTER FIVE

The Best-Laid Plans of Mice and Mousemen

General Algernon, the leader of the warlords, aimed his gleaming plasma-beam blaster squarely at Zack.

"Wow, that's the biggest ray gun I've ever seen," Zack remarked. "Can I try it?"

"No," General Algernon answered.

"Can I try your sword?"

"No!"

"Are those your real ears?"

"No! I mean, yes!"

"Why have you captured this bus?" Omega Chimp demanded. "And what have you done with Miss Canterbury?"

General Algernon fluttered his ears in annoyance. "Your Earth teachers have been insulting mice for centuries. All those stories about blind mice, mice running down clocks, tails getting chopped off." He spit out the words with disgust. "We're mad as cheddar and we're

not gonna take it anymore! One by one we are replacing all of Earth's teachers with robot duplicates who will teach all the wonders and glories of mice. And then, when all the children of Earth have learned the true superiority of mice over humans, we will return and claim Earth's moon for our own! Mmmmm . . . sweet, delicious green cheese . . ."

Zack nudged Omega Chimp. "See? Told you so."

"Error . . . error . . . error . . . ," Effie repeated.

"Somebody do something about that annoying droid!" the warlord screeched.

"Yes, sir." One of his soldiers drew his sword. "I'll cut off his tail with a carving knife."

CHAPTER SIX

I Look Pretty Tall, but My Wheels Are High

The warlord soldier raised his sword high over FE-203. "Error . . . error . . . error . . . ," Effie repeated.

Zack pointed with one finger. "You gotta hit him here, right between the F and the E-eeeyikes!" Zack snatched his finger away from the crashing sword. "I think somebody here needs a refresher course in weapon safety!"

Effie's lights started flashing in a pattern. He stopped rolling back and forth and slowly pushed himself upright. "Thank you," he said.

A mousy engineer entered from another room. "General Algernon, the substitute teacher is complete," he said. Two mouse warlords escorted a teacher from the other room.

"Leapin' leptons! It's Miss Craterbrain!" Zack cried.

"Miss Canterbury!" the children wailed.

Zack looked at the kids, puzzled. "You mean her name isn't Craterbrain? That would explain all those dirty looks she used to give me. No matter."

Zack turned to General Algernon. "Your plan will never work," he said. "Look at this wiry hair, this drooping chin, this misshapen nose. What makes you think anyone will mistake this deformed contraption for a living human being?"

"Because this is the real teacher. We're taking her with us."

"Oh," Zack said, wilting under the angry glare of Miss Craterbrain.

"Roll out the duplicate," General Algernon commanded.

"Leapin' leptons! It looks just like her!" Zack exclaimed.

SQUEAK SQUEAK SQUEAK TRUNDLE

The robot teacher's massive steel jaw creaked up and down. A squawking metallic voice scratched out from a tiny speaker behind her jaw. "Back to your seats now, children. It's time for our History of Mice lesson."

"You're not our teacher!" a blond-haired girl protested.

Twin laser blasts shot out from the robot's eyes, burning the tips of the little girl's shoes. "Back to your seats!" the robot screeched. In the blink of an eye the kids streaked like twenty meteorites back to their seats.

"Maybe we'd better turn the voltage down a bit," one of the mousy engineers said. He slipped quietly behind the teacherbot and turned a small knob on her back.

"Very good, students," the robot cooed. "Now, before we begin, would anybody like a nice, soft piece of cheese?" The robot opened a compartment in her arm and removed a plate of cheese cubes. "One for you, one for you . . ."

"You lucky space dogs!" Zack cried. "The real Miss Craterbrain never let us eat in class. Are all your teacherbots this nice?" Zack turned toward General Algernon, but the warlord leader and his mousemen were already gone.

Outside the window the fleet of cheese ships, along with Miss Craterbrai—Miss Canterbury, vanished into the darkness of space.

Is That Really Your Teacher? Don't Be Too Sure!

To find out if your teacher has been replaced by an evil alien robot duplicate, take this quick and foolproof test. *Do not* turn in this test when you are finished!

1) Does your teacher sometimes trip over her own cord?

Yes   No

2) Does your teacher have glowing red lightbulbs for eyes, a circuit breaker on her forehead, or miniature satellite dishes where her ears should be? (Note: Red eyes on Monday morning don't count. That is normal.)

Yes   No

3) Has your teacher ever said, "Just a minute, I have to reboot"?

Yes   No

4) Does your teacher ever give you homework?

Yes   No

Scoring

Score 1 point for every Yes answer. Score 2 points for answering Yes on question 4. Score 3 points if it's math homework.

Results

7–12 Check your math and try again.

4–6 Your teacher is definitely an alien robot duplicate! If you are a genuine intergalactic space hero and have access to a portable nuclear power source, you know what to do. If not, then your best hope for survival is to say nothing, but make sure you draw tiny mice on all of your assignments before turning them in.

1–3 Your teacher is *probably* an alien robot duplicate. Keep a close eye on your teacher and watch for leaking oil, rust stains, or wearing white shoes after Labor Day. Report to your school principal immediately if any of these signs occur.

0 Your teacher is not a robot duplicate. She is most likely a space alien instead. If she ever asks you questions about Earth's planetary defense systems, make up something that will scare the daylights out of her.

CHAPTER SEVEN

Follow That Mouse!

Well, they're gone," Zack said. "Looks like our work here is done."

"What do you mean, 'done'? We have to find them!" Omega Chimp replied. "They're replacing Earth's schoolteachers with evil alien robots."

"So? Who can tell the difference? And just think of the savings to taxpayers."

The children slumped in their seats as their new robot teacher droned on and on about the wonders of mice.

"We want Miss Canterbury," one of the children whimpered.

"She's a good teacher," said another child.

"She's smart and she's funny and she's nice to us."

"Nice to you!" Zack scoffed. "Try goofing off in class, not doing your homework, and calling her Miss Craterbrain for a whole year! See how nice she is then."

"But Commander, if we don't stop them, millions of space mice will eat the moon," Effie added.

"That's right, I forgot! Quick, Omega Chimp, transport us back to our ship."

"I can't," Omega Chimp answered. "The wristbands are still sitting back there on the control panel."

"Wristbands? What wristbands?"

"The wristbands we need to transport back to the ship."

"Leapin' leptons! Why didn't you tell me we needed wristbands?"

"Is there a transporter on this bus?" Omega Chimp asked a boy.

"Already found it!" Zack called, randomly flipping switches and turning dials on the transporter. "But I think it's broken."

"You're not supposed to turn the knobs," a little girl said.

"And it doesn't work unless you have the teacher key," the boy added. "They put a lock on it after some kid on a field trip went to sharpen a pencil and ended up transporting Miss Canterbury to one of Jupiter's moons."

"That was an accident!" Zack said.

With no means of returning to their ship, Zack, Effie, and Omega Chimp were forced to set out after the warlords of Nibblecheese in the school bus, taking along with them twenty second graders and one evil alien robot substitute teacher.

"Don't forget where we're parked," Zack told Omega Chimp as they left the Giant Slayer floating in space.

CHAPTER EIGHT

Next Stop, Nibblecheese

Using the map on the wall and the teacher's edition of their galactic geography textbook, the students were easily able to locate the planet Nibblecheese, and it wasn't long before Omega Chimp was piloting the school bus into orbit.

"The holovid program said the warlords' headquarters are located in Mount Parmesan, somewhere in the Nibbly Swiss Alps," Zack said.

Mount Parmesan was the tallest mountain in the Alps. Spotting a landing pad at the base of the mountain, Omega Chimp settled the school bus there alongside dozens of empty cheese-wedge fighters.

There was nobody in sight, but a giant mousehole in the side of the mountain left little doubt about where the warlords had gone.

"To the movies?" Zack offered. "No, to the library. Oh, I know—they went to the dentist! Mice have those big front teeth, so—"

They went into that hole!" Omega Chimp screamed.

Zack snapped his fingers. "Or maybe, just maybe, they went into that hole. . . ."

Effie's lights flashed in admiration. "Commander, you're a genius!"

"You kids stay here and play nice," Zack said to the students as he led Omega Chimp and Effie toward the entrance to the mountain. The robot substitute followed after them.

We can't just leave these kids out here all by themselves," Omega Chimp said.

"They're not by themselves," Zack answered. "They're with one another. Come on. let's go."

"And why is she coming with us?" Omega Chimp asked. making a face at the robot substitute. "Shouldn't she be teaching those kids about mice?"

"I'll bet she knows right where to find General Algernon." Zack said.

"Affirmative." the robot replied.

Omega Chimp reluctantly followed Zack, Effie, and the robot teacher down a long, sloping passageway that led into the mountain. Soon they reached a four-way intersection. "Which way should we go now?" Zack asked.

"Back the way we came," said Omega Chimp.

"Just follow me, students," the teacher replied in a singsong computerized voice. She rolled forward, leading Zack, Effie, and Omega Chimp deeper into the mountain. "Single file, line order, no shoving, that's good. . . ."

The teacherbot led them down the passage and turned right, then left, then made two more rights and arrived at another four-way intersection. Left, straight, right, straight, right, left, straight, left. Every hallway they went down looked just like every other one.

"Leapin' leptons!" Zack cried at last. "What a puzzling passageway, what a bewildering basement, what a confounding corridor—"

"It's a maze, you dolt!" Omega Chimp shrieked. "And we're lost in it!"

CHAPTER NINE

Mazed and Confused

Omega Chimp looked in every direction but had no idea which way was out. He glanced at the teacherbot. Her electronic eyes focused on the next bend and glowed with a sinister purpose.

Omega Chimp grabbed Zack by the arm. "She's not leading us to General Algernon's headquarters," he whispered. "She's leading us into a trap!"

"Nonsense!" Zack replied. "The warlords' headquarters could be just around this corner."

Zack turned the corner. "Bananas!" he cried, and leaped toward the pile of fruit.

Omega Chimp grabbed Zack by the ankles and pulled him back. "It's a trap, Zack! Don't touch those bananas." Omega Chimp turned to the robot substitute. "Lead us back to the surface," he demanded. "Right now!"

"It's not yet time for recess, children," the robot replied.

"Then we'll find our own way out," Omega Chimp said.

"If we try to leave, she'll blast us to space dust," Zack said.

"They turned her voltage down, remember?" Omega Chimp replied. "She wouldn't hurt a fly."

"And along the way we'll learn more about the wonderful world of mice," the teacher chimed robotically.

"But what about the bananas?" Zack asked Omega Chimp.

"Forget 'em," Omega Chimp answered.

Zack, Omega Chimp, and Effie traveled slowly back through the maze as best they could, with the evil teacher-bot lecturing close behind. "Mice are not only the most beautiful of all Earth's creatures, they are also the most intelligent," she said. "In fact . . ."

Effie looked back. With hundreds of built-in mechanical attachments, he was certain he could remove those bananas from the trap without triggering it. He quietly turned and disappeared behind the corner.

CHAPTER TEN

Don't Touch That Dial!

". . . and in addition to discovering gravity and electricity, mice pioneered space travel, created the Astronet, and invented the computer mouse," the teacherbot continued.

"She just never stops talking," Zack groaned. "She's even worse than the real Miss Craterbrain."

They reached a four-way intersection. Omega Chimp stopped and scratched his head. "I'm totally lost, Commander," he admitted. "We'll never find our way out of here."

"Keep moving, children," the substitute teacher said.

Omega Chimp took a step, and his feet flew out from under him. He spun three times in the air, flailing his arms and legs like a furry windmill in a hurricane. Then he crashed face-first to the ground.

"Stellar! Do that again!" Zack cried.

SLOW-MOTION REPLAY

Omega Chimp stuck one finger into a slippery pool on the floor. "Oil," he said. "Miss Rustbucket here is leaking every-where."

"Not everywhere," Zack corrected him. "Only in the places she's been."

Omega Chimp's face suddenly bright-ened. "That's right. And if she's been drip-ping oil the whole way, then she's left a trail leading right back to the entrance."

"School's out!" Zack said, and shoved his way past the robot substitute. She bounced backward against the wall, banging the small knob on her back.

"Stop or be annihilated!" the robot screeched.

"Look out!" Omega Chimp yelled. "Her electric brain is in overdrive!"

Zack froze. He turned around slowly, already afraid of what he would see.

The alien substitute seemed to have grown two feet taller. Her jaw was a jagged death trap of shining steel spikes. Her eyes burned with a hateful glow, and four robotic arms burst out from her sides, each outfitted with a powerful ray gun. An antenna telescoped upward from the top of her head. "General Algernon, the meddling space heroes have been taken prisoner," she croaked.

"Genuine intergalactic meddling space heroes!" Zack protested.

"Excellent," came the warlord's mousy voice through the robot's mouth speaker. "Take them to the mines. There they will join the captured teachers in digging their own prison for the rest of their lives! Mwah-ha-ha!"

CHAPTER ELEVEN

Bananas Away!

Meanwhile, Effie inched nearer to the trap and extended a long, thin mechanical arm over the bananas. A three-fingered titanium hand sprang out from the end of the arm. Effie lowered the titanium claw on a steel cable toward the bananas. As soon as the mechanical hand was level with the bananas, the three fingers closed.

Effie raised his mechanical arm, lifting the bananas ever so slightly.

Snap!

The trap sprang itself, spinning Effie in circles and sending the bananas flying.

When the dizziness wore off, Effie scanned everywhere, but all his sensors came back negative. The bananas were nowhere to be found.

Effie started down the hall after Zack and the others, then stopped. He looked back, then forward again. He peered down a side corridor. The hallways all looked the same.

"Commander Proton?" he called.

THE zzzzzzAQ FAQ!

Readers' questions answered by the second-greatest genuine intergalactic space hero of all time.

Q: You don't really believe the moon is made of green cheese, do you?

A: It is, and I can prove it. I have a real moon rock at home that I found in my refrigerator.

Q: If you're the second-greatest genuine intergalactic space hero of all time, who's the first?

A: Sam Spaceway, of course! He's the best. He's even better than Captain Carnivore. I've never met him, but when I do, I'm gonna tell him he's an interplanetary ideal, a galactic Galahad, a hyperspace Hercules! [Editor's note: At least he's not a shipless sycophant.]

Q: What's a sycophant?

A: A sycophant is an elephant with a cold. [Editor's note: No it's not.]

Q: Is Captain Carnivore a real space hero or just a made-up character in comic books and video games?

A: He's as real as you and me. The Oortian Armada wouldn't bother chasing him if he weren't real.

Q: But isn't the Oortian Armada just a gang of made-up bad guys in Captain Carnivore comics and video games?

A: Of course not! If they were just made-up bad guys, they wouldn't be a threat to Captain Carnivore, now would they?

That's all we have room for this time. Thanks for writing, everyone! See you in the next zzzzzZAQ FAQ!

CHAPTER TWELVE

You're Mine, All Mine

At the opening of a deep mine shaft, General Algernon and his mouse warlords surrounded Zack and Omega Chimp. The evil robot kept her laser beam eyes aimed squarely at Zack and Omega Chimp to prevent their escape.

"We've kidnapped so many Earth teachers we don't know where to put them all," General Algernon said. "So we're making them dig a huge underground prison."

"I'll bet they like it there," Zack said. "School always felt like prison to me."

"Good. Then you'll be happy there too."

"Me? Now wait a second, General. . . ."

General Algernon motioned to his guards, and ten mousemen wielding razor-sharp spears closed in on Zack and Omega Chimp. "Into the mines with them!" Algernon demanded.

Zack looked around for Effie, but the little droid was nowhere in sight. "Wait, we can't go! I have to find my . . ."

Zack went cross-eyed staring at the spear point that appeared in front of his nose.

"If these two space heroes are not down there in three seconds, fill them with more holes than a pound of Swiss cheese," the general commanded. "One, two . . ." His warriors leveled their spears, but Zack and Omega Chimp were already scrambling into the dark hole.

General Algernon turned to the robot substitute. "Back to the surface with you," he commanded her. "Educate those Earth children."

"Yes, General," the teacherbot replied, and obediently clanked away, her eyes glowing red with excitement.

Algernon turned back to his warriors. "Gather all the explosives from the armory," he ordered them. "That pesky spaceman and his chimpanzee friend will never leave that mine alive."

- CHEESE -

A LOVING ODE TO THE MOST DELIGHTFUL
FOOD IN ALL THE UNIVERSE
BY GENERAL ALGERNON tHE GREat!

I THINK THAT NO MOUSE EVER SEES,
A POEM AS LOVELY AS SOME CHEESE.

COOKIES? CANDY? NOT FOR ME!
GIVE ME GOUDA, SWISS, OR BRIE.

MOZZARELLA! SUCH A TREAT,
LIKE CRACKERS TO A PARAKEET.

CHEESE THAT'S YELLOW, CHEESE WITH HOLES,
STEAMING HOT CHEESE CASSEROLES!

CHEDDAR NOW AND BLUE CHEESE SOON,
THEN GREEN CHEESE FROM YOUR PLANET'S MOON

POEMS ARE MADE BY MICE WITH FLEAS
BUT I'D SURE LIKE A BITE OF CHEESE.

CHAPTER THIRTEEN

Between a Rock and a Hard Face

Zack and Omega Chimp trudged down the dark passageway into the mine. Each step took them farther into the heart of the planet Nibblecheese.

"Why did I ever take you onboard my ship?" Omega Chimp whined.

"Because deep down inside you're a genuine intergalactic space hero just like me," Zack answered.

"I'm deep down inside this planet just like you, and that's where the similarity ends!" Omega Chimp argued back. "What's so heroic about digging a giant hole for an army of insane mice?"

Zack thought for a moment. "Well, gee, Omega Chimp, when you put it that way, it hardly sounds heroic at all."

"It's not heroic!" Omega Chimp screamed.

"Then why are we doing it?" Zack asked.

The passageway widened into a vast hollow, and Zack and Omega Chimp saw two teachers banging picks and shovels against the rock walls of an enormous teachers' lounge carved out of solid rock.

Zack shoved Omega Chimp behind a boulder and crouched down beside him.

"If those schoolteachers catch us down here, they'll give us spelling words and math tests and make us sit quietly and eat our lunches," Zack whispered.

"We don't have any lunches," Omega Chimp replied.

"We would if you had let me get those bananas," Zack grumbled.

Omega Chimp watched the teachers for a moment, then made a puzzled expression. "Zack, look. Those teachers aren't really digging. They're just banging their tools together and making a lot of digging sounds."

Zack peeked around the boulder. There were only two teachers there, but they were making the noise of ten. One of the teachers glanced over and caught Zack squarely in the beam of her helmet light. Zack froze. The teacher sneakily waved Zack and Omega Chimp over.

"These teachers are up to something," Omega Chimp said, "and I don't think it involves math or spelling."

The teachers stopped their digging sounds and looked up toward the mine entrance. "Go help the other teachers in the back of the cavern," they whispered. "Hurry."

"Get back to work!" shouted a mousy voice from above. The teachers motioned for Zack and Omega Chimp to get going, and went back to banging their picks and shovels.

Near the back of the cavern dozens of teachers were working in two teams. One group of teachers was digging a tunnel that led directly toward the back of the mountain, and the other group was digging a deep pit.

"Mr. Proton!" screeched a familiar voice.

Zack looked up in horror to find Miss Craterbrain glaring down at him. "Looks like Algernon bagged himself a couple of space heroes," she said.

"What's going on here?" Omega Chimp asked.

"Those two ladies up front are fooling the guards into thinking we're widening the cavern to make room for more teachers," Miss Craterbrain explained, "but we're really tunneling our way out the back of the mountain. And just in case those mice decide to come after us, this pit should slow them down."

Zack peered into the pit. "Leapin' leptons! What a humongous hole, what a deep divide, what a voluminous void!"

"I'm glad you like it," Miss Crater-brain said, slapping mining helmets onto Zack and Omega Chimp. She thrust shovels at each of them. "Now, get down there and start digging. With your help we should be finished in about a year."

CHAPTER FOURTEEN

And Effie Makes Three

Zack scooped another shovelful of broken rocks into a bucket. "Digging through solid rock is no fun at all," he groaned. "I wish Miss Craterbrain had given us a math test instead."

"You would rather be taking a math test?" Omega Chimp asked.

"No, my personal droid always did my schoolwork for me. He's the one who would be taking the math test. Too bad Effie's not here, or he could—hey, wait a minute! I just remembered, the people of Potluck gave me that personal radio transmitter. If I can contact Effie, maybe he can do my digging for me!"

"If you can contact Effie, maybe he can get us out of here!" Omega Chimp replied.

Zack fished around in his pockets, then pulled out a miniature radio transmitter. He quickly pressed the call button. "Zack to Effie, come in, buddy."

Meanwhile, Effie had been wandering the hallways of the maze searching for Zack and Omega Chimp. He went down a hallway that ended at a door. Effie turned the knob and rolled through the doorway into a room full of armed mousemen.

"The explosives are all in place, General," one of Algernon's lieutenants announced. "We are ready to blow up the mine."

"Yikes!" cried Effie.

General Algernon and the rest of the mousemen turned.

"It's a teacher!" Algernon roared.

"No, Glorious Leader, it's a robot duplicate. That's not real hair, that's a wig."

"She's kind of cute, too, don't you think?" whispered one warlord.

Effie's lights blushed red.

Suddenly a voice cackled through Effie's radio speaker. "Zack to Effie, come in, buddy."

General Algernon looked suspiciously at Effie. One of the mousemen lifted the bananas off Effie's head with the point of a spear.

"This is no evil robot! This is a space hero in disguise!"

"I liked her better with the hair," one mouseman noted.

"Take him to the mine!" General Algernon bellowed. "And after he has joined the others, we will light the explosives and blow the mine shut forever."

CHAPTER FIFTEEN

All That Glitters

Effie glanced nervously at the explosives lining the entrance to the mine. "Perfect," General Algernon said. "Light the fuse!"

His warlords just looked at one another. "Does nobody here have a match?" Algernon bellowed.

Effie raised his hand. "I come equipped with a wide variety of built-in fire-producing devices," he offered.

Meanwhile, deep in the pit, Zack had unearthed a different sort of rock. It was smoother than the rest and heavier, and the light from Zack's helmet lamp glinted brightly off its shiny yellow surface.

"That's no ordinary rock," Omega Chimp said. "That's gold!"

"Did you say Gouda?" Zack asked. "Leapin' leptons, I was right! We've dug so deep we've struck cheese!"

At the entrance to the mine Effie lit the fuse for General Algernon and slowly rolled forward into the darkness. His radio speaker crackled to life once more as Zack's voice came through:

"Effie! Get down here! We've struck a mother lode of cheese!"

General Algernon's ears fluttered madly. "Did you hear that? Cheese! Everybody into the mine!"

General Algernon and his army of mousemen scrambled past Effie into the mine. They snatched the picks and shovels away from the startled teachers and went frantically to work, digging like madmice.

"Hurry, Commander," Effie called to Zack and Omega Chimp. "The explosives are about to blow!"

"Redshift!" Zack cried, racing from the mine. Omega Chimp and the captured teachers followed right behind him.

Miss Craterbrain was the last one out. She snatched Effie by the arm as she ran past and pulled him around the corner just as the dynamite went off with a tremendous blast. Rocks fell from above, and the mine shaft was sealed with rubble.

Help Zack and the others find their way out of Mount Parmesan!

CHAPTER SIXTEEN

Recess!

Zack was surprised by how quickly the teachers found their way back through the maze and up to the surface. "Smarter than they appear," he said. "And I mean that in a good way."

Once they reached the planet's surface, the teachers radioed the nearest
celestial sherriff's department to dig
out and arrest the trapped warlords,
then jumped into the cheese-wedge
space cruisers and sped off furiously
toward Earth. Those evil robot duplicates were in real trouble now—half of
them would be turned into high-tech
laser-powered coffeemakers in the
teachers' lounge before lunch the next
day.

Miss Craterbrain's students were gathered outside the giant mousehole playing on a playground. When they saw Miss Craterbrain, the kids all ran over and gave her a group hug.

"Where did all this come from?" Zack asked, staring at the swing set, slide, and monkey bars.

"The nice space rangers built it for us," a girl answered. "They landed while you were gone."

"They defeated the evil robot substitute and used her for parts," a boy added. "They were looking for their commander, somebody named Zack Proton."

"Leapin' leptons! That's me!"

"You fell out of your own ship?" a girl asked. "That's so funny!" The whole class broke into laughter.

"My loyal space rangers are ruining my heroic reputation!" Zack cried.

CHAPTER SEVENTEEN

A Narrow Escape

Zack, Effie, and Omega Chimp piled into the school bus ship along with Miss Craterbrain and her students and sped back to where the Giant Slayer was parked. Zack saw a small white rectangle on the windshield.

"Look, Omega Chimp. We got fan mail!" he said.

"We got a parking ticket!" Omega Chimp growled.

"Well, next time don't leave your ship in a no-floating zone," Zack said.

Miss Craterbrain used her key to unlock the transporter, and seconds later the three heroes were surrounded by a pulsating rainbow light.

"I remember this . . . ," Effie squeaked. His body started trembling, and he began singing again, "'Daisy, Daisy . . .'"

Omega Chimp started turning a sickly, fishy shade of green.

"This isn't right. Who changed all the settings?" Miss Craterbrain demanded. "Mr. Proton!" she roared.

Zack was saved by a sudden flash of light. An instant later Zack, Effie, and Omega Chimp were back on board the Giant Slayer.

"Whew! She almost got me that time!" Zack said.

"Error . . . error . . . error . . . ," Effie repeated as he rolled back and forth on the floor.

Omega Chimp just moaned, still curled up in a furry ball on the floor.

"This is no time for games, Omega Chimp," Zack said. "We've got to find the Risky Rascal." He slammed the Giant Slayer into high gear, and the ship jumped forward.

"Error . . . error . . . error!"

"Ooof!"

"Stop clowning around, you two," Zack said. "We've got a mission here, remember? Try to behave like proper space heroes for once.

"You don't think my space rangers told anybody else about me falling out of my ship, do you? Just wait'll I catch up with my ship!"

"Oh, I can't wait," Omega Chimp replied with a smile. "I really can't."

Omega Chimp fell into a happy daydream, and a second later the Giant Slayer disappeared into the blackness of space.

Gori Blastinov

Совершенно Секретно

FROM: Secret Agent Sobachka
TO: Russian Space Agency Headquarters
IMPORTANT NEWS: American hooligan boy ruined chimpanzee rocket launch today. We can still win space race. Use big male gorilla from Moscow Zoo. He is grouchy and drinks too much mango juice. Hurry, comrades!